Val had a tin of pins.

Val had a bag of pegs.

Val was in bed.

The pins and the pegs got up.

The pins and the pegs had fun.

Let's bop on the lid of the bin!
Rum tum tum!
Bim bam bom!

Val got up.

The pins and the pegs
ran and hid.

Did I put the pins in a pot? Did I put the pegs in a jug?